PENCIL

A Story with a Point

Ann Ingalls • Dean Griffiths

pajamapress

First published in Canada and the United States in 2019

10 9 8 7 6 5 4 3 2 1

 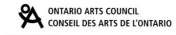

Canada Council   Conseil des arts
for the Arts   du Canada

ONTARIO ARTS COUNCIL
CONSEIL DES ARTS DE L'ONTARIO
an Ontario government agency
un organisme du gouvernement de l'Ontario

Canada

The publisher gratefully acknowledges the support of the Canada Council for the Arts and the Ontario Arts Council for its publishing program. We acknowledge the financial support of the Government of Canada through the Canada Book Fund (CBF) for our publishing activities.

Library and Archives Canada Cataloguing in Publication

Ingalls, Ann, author
          Pencil : a story with a point / Ann Ingalls ; Dean Griffiths, illustrator. -- First edition.
ISBN 978-1-77278-047-5 (hardcover)
          I. Griffiths, Dean, 1967-, illustrator II. Title.
PZ7.I45Pen 2019   j813'.6   C2018-903832-2

Publisher Cataloging-in-Publication Data (U.S.)

Names: Ingalls, Ann, author. | Griffiths, Dean, 1967-, illustrator.
Title: Pencil : A Story With a Point / Ann Ingalls, Dean Griffiths.
Description: Toronto, Ontario Canada : Pajama Press, 2018. | Summary: "Relegated to the junk drawer after his boy Jackson becomes enamored with a new tablet, Pencil rallies his fellow tools and office supplies in a pun-punctuated text. Together, they find a creative way to catch Jackson's attention: a flipbook created using their many combined talents"—— Provided by publisher.
Identifiers: ISBN 978-1-77278-047-5 (hardcover)
Subjects: LCSH: Computers — Juvenile fiction. | Friendship — Juvenile fiction. | Puns and punning — Juvenile fiction. | BISAC: JUVENILE FICTION / Social Themes / Values & Virtues. | JUVENILE FICTION / Imagination & Play. | JUVENILE FICTION / Computers & Digital Media.
Classification: LCC PZ7.I543Pe | DDC [E] — dc23

Original art created digitally
Cover and book design—Rebecca Bender

Manufactured by Qualibre Inc./Printplus
Printed in China

Pajama Press Inc.
181 Carlaw Ave. Suite 251 Toronto, Ontario Canada, M4M 2S1

Distributed in Canada by UTP Distribution
5201 Dufferin Street Toronto, Ontario Canada, M3H 5T8

Distributed in the U.S. by Ingram Publisher Services
1 Ingram Blvd. La Vergne, TN 37086, USA

For Susie Henton and Karen Wenban, two
teachers who changed lives with a bit of chalk
and some encouragement

—Ann

For Rebecca, who loves pencils

—Dean

Pencil and Jackson were best friends.
They went everywhere together.

They scribbled and sketched.
They played mustache,
airplane,
and parade.
They had loads of fun until...

...Tablet moved in.

Jackson was captivated by Tablet!

CAN YOU MAKE MOVIES?

Tablet asked Pencil.

CAN YOU DRAW IN COLOR?

CAN YOU MESSAGE GRANDMA IN SOUTH DAKOTA? HMMMM?

Pencil had been #1.
Now he felt like #2.

One day when Jackson was
playing with Tablet,
he dropped Pencil on the floor.
Bernie picked him up and
nearly chewed him to bits.

Pencil was covered with teeth
marks and drool.
And then it happened, the
final disgrace...

Jackson tossed Pencil into the
junk drawer. It looked like
Pencil would live out his life
with a jumble of junk,
lost and forgotten.
Everything in that drawer was
blunt or broken.

Pencil couldn't see any point
in going on.

Pencil nearly lost his grip.

Every time someone opened the drawer,
Pencil pushed his way to the top,
hoping he'd be chosen.
Then one day, it happened.

Jasmine opened the drawer.

Pencil was free at last!

Pencil traveled everywhere on Jasmine's head.
Once in a while, Pencil and Jasmine sat with Tablet.

TABLET, CAN'T WE JUST GET ALONG?

asked Pencil.

GET LOST! YOU'RE NOT MY TYPE!

said Tablet.

The very next day...

MASH!

Bernie knocked
Tablet on the floor.

NO MORE VIDEOS?
NO MORE GAMES?
NO MORE MOVIES?

A tear rolled down Jackson's cheek.

Pencil was stumped.

WHAT CAN I
DO?

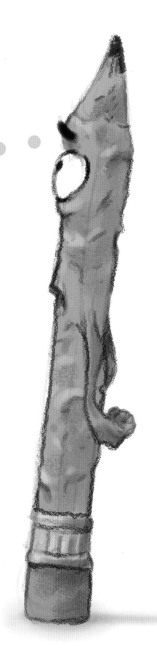

He went back to the junk drawer for help.

He tried on pencil toppers with fuzzy hair,

with glitz,

with springs,

with googly eyes.

Nothing worked.

A pencil with an eraser on each end is just pointless.

But Pencil was sharp!

Pencil showed Jackson all the
other cool things he could do.
He could be a bookmark.
He could be a back scratcher.
He could be a tent pole for a
really small tent.

None of this
worked either.

Then Pencil had a new idea.
He went back to the junk drawer
to see if Sticky Notes would help.
Pencil sketched his idea.

HE'LL GET A REAL
CHARGE OUT OF
THAT,

said Battery.

Pencil and his friends began to create a fancy flip-book.

HAPPY TO HOLD THINGS TOGETHER,

said Paper Clip and Tape.

Jackson picked up
Pencil and began
to draw.

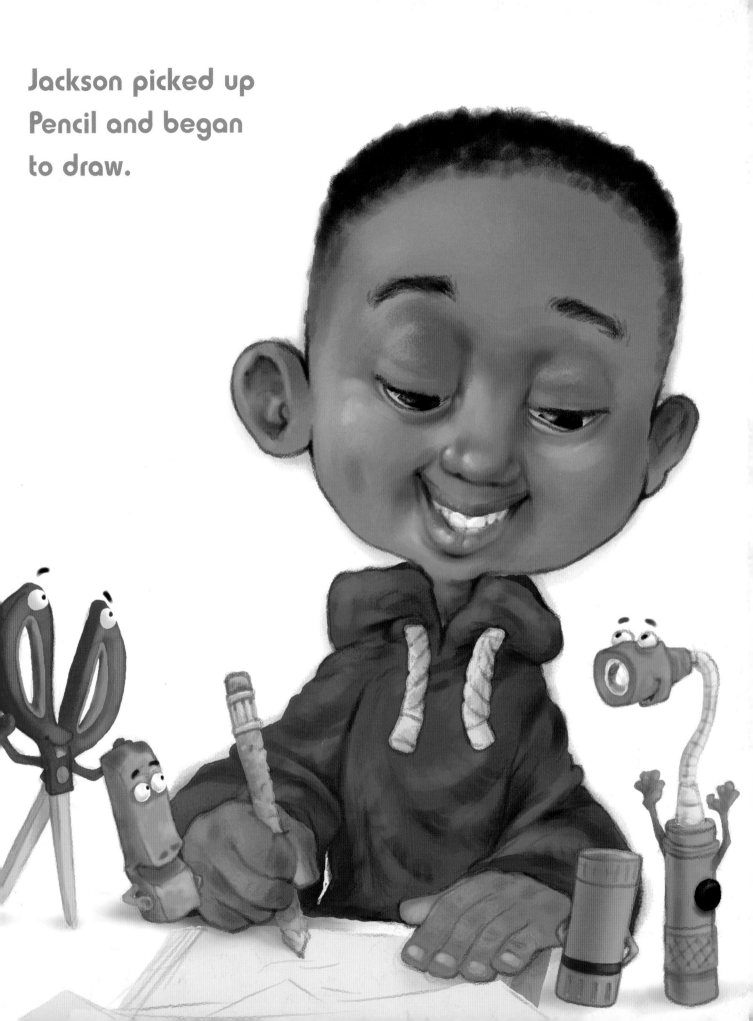

WHAT WOULD
I DO WITHOUT
ALL OF YOU?

asked Pencil.

WE STICK
TOGETHER,

said Glue.